Secrets In My Face

Enchantments That Bind

To CASH
Enjoy the Secrets
[signature]

By

Ronald Wayne Capodagli, Jr.

Dedication

To my wife Jan, your passion for reading has influenced me to write this book for you all. And to my children, it is my hope that when your children are old enough, this book will be the first of many ghost story tales in their lives. As you take this book off the shelf, dust it off, and read the stories within to your children - let their spirits be carried by their imagination.

Acknowledgment

I would like to express my deep gratitude to my customers for their patience as I serviced and repaired their "enchanted" clocks. I would also like to thank my grandmother for her many "scary" stories she shared with me as I was growing up. My grateful thanks are also extended to my teachers, who nurtured my daydreaming into creative writing.

Finally, I wish to thank my wife for her support and encouragement throughout the writing of this enchanted book.

About the Author

I have spent a lifetime raising the standards of excellence in my 40-year history of personal projects of crafting, repairing, and building an assortment of clocks. This book allows me to share with you just a ghostly enchantment that had occurred in my shop in years past. Since then, I have learned to appreciate that there is much more to a clock than the crafting, servicing, and repairing. Who could have imagined that in these activities, ghostly enchantments would be a part of this clock's history for years to come.

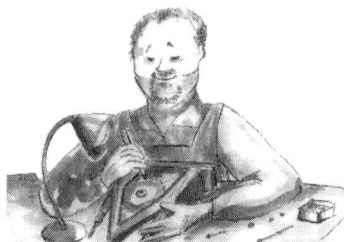

Preface

The enchantment presented in this book really happened; many of the experiences were of my own. The rest are from stories my grandmother shared—I share the same passion to bring this story into your home on that very special dark and dreary night.

The Old Oak Clock

It was a beautiful Monday morning when the doorbell chimed, announcing the arrival of the day's first customer.

"Good morning. Welcome to Clocks and Quilts. How may I help you?" Mr. Wayne brightly said to the old lady as she was coming in with a worn bag in her hand.

"I would like a very special timepiece looked at please. Sadly, it no longer keeps time," she said in a shaky, breathy voice, struggling with each step towards the store counter.

"No problem. Let's put the watch on the counter."

The old lady nodded and then pulled out a small black velvet box from her bag. Inside was a beautiful, fancy wristwatch with exotic rhinestones on the dial.

"This is quite a collectible you have." Mr. Wayne inspected the watch for a few moments and then looked up at the old lady again. "Don't worry. It can be easily fixed. Please come by tomorrow and I will have your watch ready and keeping good time again."

"Thank you," she said as she turned around to head for the door - only to pause for a moment as an amber-studded clock sitting proudly on the shelf caught her eye.

"Would you like to get that clock for your home? We just got it delivered yesterday." Mr. Wayne carefully pointed at the clock sitting in the middle of the many shelves that covered almost all four walls of the shop. All were filled with clocks of different shapes, sizes, and colors. The particular one he was pointing at was an exquisite clock indeed, and it was no surprise that it caught the old lady's eye.

"No, thank you. I will come by tomorrow and collect my watch." She said abruptly, averting her gaze.

"Sure, ma'am. I'll look forward to your visit. Thank you," Mr. Wayne said politely.

Mr. Wayne had been in the clock business for as long as he could remember. It was what his father before him did, and so did his grandfather. They were the most well-known clockmakers in the area, and the name Clocks and Quilts was an authentic and trusted one. But for the last few months, the shop hadn't been doing so well, so Mr. Wayne was trying his best to market the many clocks he and his family had collected over the years.

Maybe I'll show her the amber-studded clock tomorrow. If it got her attention from afar, then from up close she would really like it, Mr. Wayne thought to himself, as the old woman seemed very interested in the clock. Mr. Wayne put the velvet box inside the drawer under the counter. He would fix it later. Just as he closed the drawer, the doorbell chimed again. Mr. Wayne looked up to see an old man looking distressed as he entered the shop. In his hands was an old oak clock.

"Welcome to Clocks and Quilts. How may I help you?"

An old man shakily walked up to the counter. His clothes were extremely crinkled, like they hadn't been ironed in ages, and his hair looked like he just got out of bed. Mr. Wayne couldn't help to notice that the man standing across Mr. Wayne's counter fit the description of someone the townspeople called "Old Burt". Though there had been many stories told in his neighborhood about Old Burt, he had never seen Old Burt in person… Well, that was up till now.

"Hi, I'm Burt," uttered the man before putting the old oak clock cradled in his hands on top of the counter.

"That is a beautiful old clock. Would you like it to be serviced?" Mr. Wayne asked.

"Oh no, it works perfectly fine. I'm here to sell it." The man tried to pass a smile, but the beads of sweat on his forehead showed he was anything but happy right now.

"I'm sorry, Mr. Burt. But I'm not buying any clocks right now." Mr. Wayne returned a sympathetic smile. His shop was already filled with so many clocks. Buying any, now, wouldn't do him any good. So he had paused that part of the business for now until his clocks started selling again.

"What? Surely you can make an exception? You haven't even looked at it. It's a rare piece." He took the clock in his hands and fumbled with it, trying to show it to Mr. Wayne from every angle.

"Yes, you are very right, Sir. It is indeed is a unique piece. Might even be an antique, I would guess." He looked at the wooden clock, and for sure, the clock looked like one that would be of great value. The intricate design carved on its oak wood was not something that was typically found in wall clocks these days. "But, I'm afraid I can't buy this clock from you. As you can see, I already filled my shop with so many clocks that need to be sold. I simply can't accept any more because I don't have the space for them. I am very sorry."

Old Burt started to get impatient as he put the clock back down on the counter with hands that were now shaking.

"Then how about you keep it on consignment?" Old Burt blurted out.

"Can I ask you the reason you want to sell this clock so badly?" Mr. Wayne asked.

"I will be moving soon, and I won't need this clock anymore. So, I just want to get rid of, I mean, sell it," he corrected himself.

Mr. Wayne thought in silence for a few seconds before he spoke again.

"OK, I'll do what I can for you and keep the clock on consignment," he announced, and as if Old Burt had been holding it in, he exhaled a deep breath.

"Thank you, thank you," Old Burt said.

"Would you like to look at new options now that you are getting rid of the old one?" Mr. Wayne asked.

"No, no. As I said, I won't need a clock anymore," he replied and made his way out of the shop, leaving the old clock behind.

"Hey Jennie, I'm here." Mr. Wayne called out as he made his way into his house after closing the shop for the day.

Mrs. Wayne rushed up to Mr. Wayne to greet him.

"How was your day?" she asked.

"It was busier than usual, or rather peculiar, I'd say." He sat down on the couch and put a bag that he brought from the shop on the table.

"Peculiar? How so?" Mrs. Wayne took her place beside him as Mr. Wayne told her the entire event about Old Burt visiting the shop and leaving his clock behind.

"It's in this bag. There wasn't any place in the shop I could've put this, so I brought it home for now. Tomorrow I will go in early and clean some of the old junk out of the shop so I can find a place to put this clock."

Mrs. Wayne opened the bag and took out the old oak clock out of it. She gasped loudly.

"It is very beautiful. Very sophisticated and elegant," she observed. Mr. Wayne himself was shocked after he saw how beautiful the clock came out after he had cleaned it.

"I know! And can you believe it? He gave it to me to sell on consignment," Mr. Wayne remarked.

"Wow, can we buy it?" She wasn't able to take her eyes off the clock.

It was love at first sight, you could say.

"Sure, if you like it that much. I was going to have to clean up the shop to make space for it." Mr. Wayne laughed.

"Well, if you are going to put off the cleaning because of it, I should probably let you keep the clock," Mrs. Wayne joked, and they both laughed.

Later, before going to bed, Mrs. Wayne hung the clock next to the bookshelf in her sewing room, where she would often go to spend some time quilting when she would get restless at night.

The next day, when Mr. Wayne went to the shop just like every day, Mrs. Wayne busied herself in the kitchen. She was boiling some potatoes for dinner, and as she was straining them, she heard a loud thumping coming from the sewing room. Wondering what was causing the sound, as there was no one in the house besides her, she deduced that she must've left the TV on.

She went to the living room after leaving the potatoes to cool, and she saw that the TV was turned off. Thinking that she must've imagined the sound all along, as she couldn't hear it anymore, she went back into the kitchen.

That evening, when it was about time for Mr. Wayne to come home, she went to the sewing room to piece a block or two of her favorite quilt and sip some hot tea since she was tired from working in the kitchen the whole day. Moreover, she had heard the thumping sound too many times. She moved around the entire house, but wasn't able to locate its source. She figured it would be better to relax a little before her husband came home.

As soon as she entered the sewing room and turned on the light, her eyes fell to the place where she had last hung the wooden clock.

It was not there.

She perfectly remembered hanging the clock

on the wall next to the bookshelf, but it couldn't be found anywhere in the room. After scanning the whole room, she found the clock sitting in the corner, under some old fabric that she used for many of her other quilts.

How did the clock get here? Mrs. Wayne was really puzzled.

She hadn't even been in the room since she had hung that clock on the wall next to the shelf shelf last night, so how was the clock sitting in the corner, under some old fabric?

It made little sense.

When Mr. Wayne got home from the shop, tired, having sold the amazing amber-studded piece that was one of the most special clocks he had ever serviced, he was really happy. After dinner, when they both settled in bed for the night,

Mrs. Wayne told him about the incident with the clock. She put the clock back on the wall next to the bookshelf, but she was still really spooked. After hearing her story, Mr. Wayne said that she must've gotten up to sew during the night and for some reason, perhaps the ticking of the clock, took the clock off the wall and covered it with the old fabric and had forgotten to put it back.

"Looks like someone's getting older," joked Mr. Wayne. Mrs. Wayne pretended to laugh, but in reality, she could feel that something was wrong.

The next day, just like the day before, the thumping noise started after Mr. Wayne left. This time Mrs. Wayne was terrified to go into the sewing room, in fear of where else she might find the clock. However, she mustered up a little courage and walked toward the sewing room, tiptoeing when she neared the entrance. She lightly extended her hand, pulled the door by the knob, and closed it. The rest of the day, she tried her best to ignore the thumping sound and not let it get to her.

Later that the evening, when Mrs. Wayne heard a knock at the door, for a moment, she had thought it was the loud thumping that had haunted her for days now. Realizing that it was someone knocking at the front door, Mrs. Wayne rushed, hoping her husband had finally come home. As she opened the door, she was surprised to find a young woman with a small baby sleeping in her arms.

"Hello, how may I help you?" Mrs. Wayne asked, puzzled.

"Hi, I am Lisa and this is my daughter Julie." The woman spoke up. "We have been traveling for days, but have not been unable to find any shelter. We just lost our apartment and have nowhere to go."

"Have you contacted the local shelter?" Mrs. Wayne asked.

"Yes, I have. But they said that it would take a while for them to find us a place to stay, and even then, I am fearful that they would probably want to take my baby away from me. The kind folks in the shelter provided me your name and address as being someone who has helped others in similar situations and that you may be able to help us? Can you please let me stay with you for a few days until I find a place for me and Julie? Please, I don't want to be separated from my child!" Lisa pleaded.

Mrs. Wayne didn't have any children of her own, so she understood the pain to be devoid of the blessing of a child. Lisa's and Julie's clothes were very much wrinkled, but both were dressed in clean clothes. It was evident that Lisa's story and plea for help were sincere. She and her baby were indeed two people who Mrs. Wayne actually wanted to help.

Mrs. Wayne stayed quiet for a minute, trying to process everything, and she took a big breath before she spoke.

"Yes Dear, it's fine. You and Julie can stay with us for as long as you need. We have plenty of room. It's just me and my husband here, and I am sure he won't have any issues letting you and your baby stay with us."

Lisa thanked her many times as Mrs. Wayne welcomed her into the house and showed them to the guest bedroom.

Mrs. Wayne felt pretty happy, having the chance to help someone who had nowhere to go.

She was really looking forward to Lisa and her baby staying at their house.

The Consignment

Lisa took very little time to get herself and the baby settled into the house. The first day when Mr. Wayne came home and he saw the pair of them, Lisa and her baby, he felt a bit skeptical about the whole move in thing. Although he didn't say anything, you could tell from his face that he had some reservations.

"Do you really think it's a good idea to have two strangers living in our house?" He asked later when he and his wife were alone in their bedroom.

"I have a strong feeling they are good people. And honestly, I couldn't turn them away, honey. Lisa's plea touched my heart." Mrs. Wayne replied and then whispered, looking into Mr. Wayne's eyes. "And when I looked at the baby, I just couldn't say no."

Mr. Wayne's eyes softened as he listened. "Okay, if you feel that it's the right thing to do," Mrs. Wayne nodded, "I suppose it could be good for us. I have to admit I liked how our empty house is feeling livelier than usual today." Mr. Wayne added and then smiled at his lovely wife, kissing her gently on the cheek.

And just like they had hoped, as the weeks flew by, Lisa and her baby became the perfect house guests. Mrs. Wayne's highlight of the day was when she could play the role of grandmother to baby Julie, who was so well-mannered and polite.

As time went on and the relationship between Mrs. Wayne, Lisa and baby Julie grew stronger, so did the eerie sound that poured out of the sewing room each and every day. For the most part, since the arrival of Lisa and Julie, they and Mrs. Wayne rarely took notice of the occasional pounding. Mrs. Wayne and Lisa were all too busy throughout the day, taking care of and playing with baby Julie. And as it turned out, Lisa turned out to be a great help in the kitchen, with her new recipes. In no time, Mr. and Mrs. Wayne had become huge fans of Lisa's pecan pie.

"This recipe is somewhat of a family heirloom," Lisa proudly said at the dinner table, as they were all enjoying their special pecan pie slice.

"Well, let me just say that this pie is the best that I've tasted in ages!" Mr. Wayne eagerly spoke up.

"Thank you, you are too kind, sir," Lisa replied happily.

Later, when everyone had finished eating, Lisa approached Mrs. Wayne as she began collecting the dishes from the table.

"Mrs. Wayne?" she called out. Mrs. Wayne paused for a moment on her way to the kitchen to listen to her.

"Yes?" she questioned.

"When you have a moment, can I talk to you?" she asked hesitantly.

"Oh of course, I'm listening." She smiled.

"It's about your sewing room."

The smile disappeared from Mrs. Wayne's

face immediately. "What about it?" she asked cautiously.

"Um, I don't think it's my place to ask for favors, and you can say no if you want to."

"What happened in the sewing room, Lisa?" Mrs. Wayne asked impatiently. She was getting a bit nervous at this point. She hadn't gone to the room for a few days now, and the last time she went in was when she hung the clock onto the wall next to the bookshelf. Mrs. Wayne's imagination of what could be wrong was sparked by remembering how she found the clock the last time she was in the sewing room, mysteriously off the wall and hidden under one of her quilts.

"Well, how do I put this? The sewing room makes loud noises every day. And our room is right next to your sewing room, so I was wondering if you would be okay if we could investigate what is making this horrible sound."

Mrs. Wayne quickly responded, "I know it sounds stupid. It is a clock in the sewing room that is making that noise. I was very skeptical about it at first too, but one night when baby Julie woke up crying, I realized it was because of the sound from the sewing room."

Mrs. Wayne took a moment to comprehend everything, admitting that the noise might cause Lisa and baby Julie to leave. This was something Mrs. Wayne wanted to avoid at all costs.

"What? Are you sure it was the clock?" Lisa feigned surprise. "I have heard there was some construction work going on a few houses down. It could be just that." She gave a nervous chuckle.

"No, Lisa. I am sure that it was coming from the clock in my sewing room."

Lisa took a deep breath while thinking that

Mrs. Wayne sure was hesitant about all that she was sharing with her.

"Let's see what is going on with the clock." Mrs. Wayne continued. "We sure don't want you or baby Julie to feel unconfrontable in our home."

Lisa thanked her and went back to her room. Now, Mrs. Wayne had to get the clock out of the room, and it was something she was dreading. Presuming Mr. Wayne was already half-asleep, she decided that she would have to do it alone. She quietly made her way to the sewing room and standing right in front of the door, she took in a few deep breaths before she opened it.

The room was completely submerged in darkness and Mrs. Wayne could not see a thing from the small crack of a slightly opened door. She reached through the opening, feeling her way to the light, and turned it on. The room illuminated with white light and Mrs. Wayne cautiously stepped inside, pushing the door as far open as it would go.

She looked beside the bookshelf. The clock was not there, just as she feared.

After a few moments of searching, Mrs. Wayne was startled to find the clock on the floor behind the door. It was as if the clock was waiting there for someone to come in. *Why?* She wondered.

She cautiously knelt down and picked the old oak clock in her hands. Mrs. Wayne felt a sense of peace as she cradled the clock in her arms. She turned around and left the sewing room, closing the door behind her. Mrs. Wayne decided to take the clock to her bedroom, as it was the only other room she felt comfortable putting it in.

Mr. Wayne was fast asleep on the bed, so she quickly joined him after carefully hanging the clock on the wall using a nail that once supported an old portrait.

The old oak clock was peacefully quiet, so much so that Mrs. Wayne was able to go to sleep thinking that maybe her suspicions about the clock were wrong all along and it was all part of her imagination. *Perhaps her husband had put the clock under the quilt and then behind the door? But why would he do that? And it still doesn't explain the noises...* she wondered as she fell into a deep slumber.

Mrs. Wayne woke up in the middle of the night with a startle.

"Honey, what's wrong?" Mr. Wayne quickly asked after being woken up.

"It's okay. I just had a bad dream. Go back to sleep," she said, although Mrs. Wayne looked anything but okay.

"You look pale." Mr. Wayne replied as he poured her a glass of water from a bottle on his bedside table. "Here, take a sip."

Mrs. Wayne took the glass from his hands and drank the water.

"Feeling better now?" Mr. Wayne asked. She nodded in a gracious response.

They both went back to sleep, and there was no further incident that night. However, for Mrs.

Wayne, it was just a beginning of a series of nightmares, all where she saw the old clock ticking away, causing her to wake up in fear. After four days of sleepless nights, she couldn't bear the nightmares anymore, and decided to share her dreams with Mr. Wayne.

"So, you are saying that the clock used to make noises, and now it's giving you nightmares?" he asked after hearing her story.

"Yes, and believe me, it's real. I'm not making anything up." She cried.

"Of course I believe you, Honey." He pondered for a few moments while Mrs. Wayne softly sobbed. "Now that I think about it, that old man (Burt) was actually way too eager to sell the clock to me. I thought it very suspicious that he even gave it to me on consignment when I wouldn't buy it from him."

"You think he knew that there was something wrong with it?" Mrs. Wayne asked.

"I think he was very well aware of the clock's enchantments. And old Burt doesn't really have a great reputation. He may very well have an agenda of his own that does not favor us or the clock." Mr. Wayne continued after a pause. "I think I need to go find him. He might have the answers that we are looking for."

The next day Mr. Wayne called every shop owner in town and asked them if Old Burt had tried to sell them some of his trinkets in the past. Some of the other shop owners responded that he was actually trying to sell them a clock, an old oak clock. Mr. Wayne then tried to contact the local shelter and a few hotels around town to ask if they were aware of Old Burt's whereabouts, but received the same answer. He was not there, nor had they seen him.

At the end of the day, Mr. Wayne was extremely frustrated, as he still had no clue that could lead him to Old Burt. The last place he visited was the police station, and he was glad that he did because the police knew about Old Burt's whereabouts.

Unfortunately, Mr. Wayne would not be able to contact him or question him, as Old Burt had passed away alone.

It turned out that Old Burt had mysteriously drowned in an old well near the town's cemetery, coincidently on the same day he had brought the old oak clock to Mr. Wayne's shop.

Old Burt

Learning about Old Burt's death and on the same day he received the old oak clock on consignment was very unsettling to Mr. Wayne. There was something about the incident that didn't sit right and Mr. Wayne realized his day's worth of investigation might lead to some deeper, hidden secrets.

"When will the funeral take place?" Mr. Wayne asked the police sergeant who informed him of Old Burt's death.

"Day after tomorrow, 10 a.m. at the town's church," said the sergeant dismissively.

"Thank you," Mr. Wayne replied as he turned around to head out of the police station.

As he was walking out of the police station, Mr. Wayne wondered if Old Burt had any family. There hadn't been anyone in town that knew of anyone related to Old Burt, nor did anyone have any idea of where he had actually been living? And now that Old Burt wasn't alive anymore, it would be extremely difficult to get answers to all the questions that Mr. Wayne was asking.

In any case, if he was going to get any answers, it would be at the funeral. If anything, it would be a great place to start since he had no idea in which direction to head.

Mr. Wayne arrived at his home feeling

unaccomplished and tired when Mrs. Wayne opened the door to greet him, her face full of questions that she believed he might now know the answers to.

"Did you find him?" Mrs. Wayne impatiently asked, as Mr. Wayne settled onto the sofa.

"No, I didn't. And I won't," he responded.

"What do you mean?" Mrs. Wayne asked, puzzled.

"Well, after I had searched every place I could think of, without any luck, I decided to go to a police station to ask if they knew anything when I learned that Old Burt had passed away," Mr. Wayne explained.

"WHAT?" Mrs. Wayne shouted.

"Yes, I was pretty shocked to hear it, too." He took a sip of the water Mrs. Wayne had gotten for him before he continued. "And apparently, he died by drowning mysteriously in the well at the end of town, on the same day he came into my shop to sell me the old oak clock."

"This makes no sense," Mrs. Wayne said as she settled down on the sofa next to Mr. Wayne.

"Yes, I know. I thought about it all on the way home, and I believe that it may have been a case of foul play," Mr. Wayne said, his face tense.

"What makes you think that?" Mrs. Wayne questioned, feeling more and more lost by the minute.

"Well, it was something that he said the day he came to the shop, his last day alive." Mr. Wayne paused for a moment. "When he gave me the old oak clock, he said that he would not have a need for a clock anymore." He looked at Mrs. Wayne in the eyes. "What did he mean by that?"

"Oh! This is all so terrible. What a misfortune!" said Mrs. Wayne, exasperatingly.

"You should settle down, honey. Don't worry about it too much." Mr. Wayne helped his wife up and walked her to her favorite chair in the library. She hadn't had a good night's sleep for a few days now. It was also good to know that Lisa was around to help her with a few of the daily chores, letting Mrs. Wayne spend more time resting.

"I will be going to his funeral the day after tomorrow, and hopefully, I'll be able to find out something about this," Mr. Wayne said as he sat her down. "You don't worry yourself over this."

As Mr. Wayne headed out of the library, he bumped into Lisa.

"I'm sorry, sir. How have you been doing?" Lisa asked politely.

"I'm good, thank you. But I'm afraid Mrs. Wayne is feeling a little tired," he said. "Can you look after her a bit for me? She does tend to worry about the silliest things."

"Of course, sir. That's the least I could do," Lisa immediately responded. "I'll go ask her if she needs anything." She excused herself and disappeared inside the library.

I might have to take a moment or two myself, Mr. Wayne thought as he settled onto the sofa. *I'm feeling slightly overwhelmed as well.*

More was on Mr. Wayne's mind other than the mystery of Old Burt's death. Two days passed with the endless nightmares that haunted Mrs. Wayne each night. Mr. Wayne felt helpless in bringing comfort to Mrs. Wayne's sleepless nights.

On the day of the funeral, Mr. Wayne dressed early in the morning, deciding to let his shop stay closed for the day. When he arrived at the church, he was surprised to find a small crowd of people gathered there. *Odd*, he thought, since Old Burt didn't have any known relatives, let alone friends to speak of.

The service went smoothly, and Mr. Wayne saw some familiar faces at the church. As he walked among those paying their respects, he asked many of them about Old Burt, only to find out that no one knew much about him. This left

Mr. Wayne feeling very sad that his life had ended in such a tragic way, and very surprised that there were so many present to pay their respects.

Mr. Wayne kept engaging folks, talking to different men and women, asking them if they knew anything about Old Burt. Time and time again, he didn't find out much, but learned one troubling fact. Old Burt used to plead with folks to let him hide inside their houses, screaming out that a strange man named "Larry" was out to get him.

Though this information didn't explain much, it did help Mr. Wayne understand that Old Burt was experiencing some irrational fears and thought that his life was in imminent danger.

Was it because of the old oak clock? Is that why he wanted to get rid of it so badly?

But if that was the case, why did he die when he got rid of it?

His head hurt with so many questions running through it, and Mr. Wayne thought that he might lose his senses just like Old Burt did if he didn't get home soon. Mr. Wayne paid his respects and said his goodbyes to everyone at the church, deciding to skip the burial.

When he got home, he laid on his bed, trying to rest a little, but couldn't as his mind was on nothing but Old Burt and his clock. After fidgeting around for half an hour, he looked at the old oak clock himself, seeing what was it about an old oak clock that instilled so many fears.

He took the clock off the wall and sat on his bed, carefully examining it from front to back. On the surface, there was nothing peculiar or different about the clock. It was just an old oak clock that had a delicate design to it.

When he turned the clock to look at the back

of it, the initials "PL" were artistically carved at the bottom. This gave Mr. Wayne an idea. The letters "PL" might stand for the name of the clockmaker that crafted the clock. If he could find out about the clockmaker, then maybe it would lead to a clue as to how Old Burt acquired the clock and what made it so different from other clocks.

Mr. Wayne contacted all the clockmakers that he knew, one by one, asking them if they knew someone with the initials "PL" that crafted old oak - clocks. After a few hours of calling, an old friend of his dad told him that he knew of a clockmaker named "Petri Lapera," who used to craft oak clocks like the one he had described.

When Mr. Wayne asked him what else he knew about the clockmaker named Petri Lapera, he said that, aside from clock making, Petri was also involved in other woodworks, like furniture-making. All his pieces were elegant, enchanting, one of a kind and were in much demand until the day that everyone learned a horrible truth about him.

Though he crafted all of his work with his own hands with precision, it was discovered that Petri would purchase the exotic wood from the local funeral director; swapping out the exotic caskets for pine boxes after the wake, using the wood from the exotic caskets for the crafting of his work—like the old oak clock.

The Curse

After learning the horrible truth about Petri Lapera, Mr. Wayne spent sleepless nights staring at the ceiling of his room. He found it hard to comprehend, being a clockmaker himself, that someone would have the nerve to do something so horrible and outrageous. A dead person's soul should be respected, and using the wood from their casket was a crime so heinous that Mr. Wayne was not sure he would ever be able to wrap his mind around.

With the mystery of the enchanted clock solved, Mr. Wayne was still confused as to why Old Burt wanted to get rid of the clock so badly. It sure had a terrible history behind it, nevertheless, it was a beautiful and enchanting clock.

These results of Mr. Wayne's investigation didn't end with the old clock maker. Mr. Wayne continued with his relentless search to find more about the clocks that Petri Lapera made. After a few days of asking around, meeting with people that he hadn't seen in a long, long time, Mr. Wayne uncovered something unexpected and extraordinary. The town had a terrible secret that few ever talked about, even to this day; a secret known as *the curse of the widow of Trego Court.*

This curse was widely known among most of the old folks in town, and only a few of the young people had heard rumors of it. You see, the casket that was used to make the old oak clock, the very same one in Mr. Wayne's house right now, actually belonged to the widow of Trego Court, a victim of unscrupulous behaviour by her husband in, what the townsfolk gossip would reveal as, a miserable marriage. The widow of Trego Court also suffered from many of the horrible occurrences, very similar to the ones that were going on inside Mr. Wayne's house right now.

After the wake of the widow of Trego Court—the immoral actions of the funeral director and the local clockmaker most likely set the curse into action. As the story has been told in years past, the director and clockmaker were preparing to move the widow of Trego Court from a stately oak and brass casket and into an impoverished pine box—when suddenly the widow of Trego Court woke up. What happened next is so horrifying, it is difficult to even speak of today. The director and clockmaker, without hesitation, ended the life of the widow of Trego Court—continuing with the exchange of the caskets, without a blink of an eye. People had deduced that just before widow of Trego Court had taken her last breath, she cursed the casket she was pulled from. A curse that would enchant the oak wood and anything made from it with terrible misfortunes.

After learning about the curse, an alarm went off in Mr. Wayne's head. What a brutal ending, he thought. Was this curse instrumental in what had happened to Old Burt? Everyone knew that Old Burt, one without a house or a family, lived a misfortunate life, but was that the consequence of him owning the oak clock? But then what about the man named "Larry"? The one who Old Burt was reportedly running from.

Mr. Wayne's imagination had seemed to be

fleeting. He knew he needed to and re-focus his investigation on Larry since the truth of the old clock was now uncovered. Mr. Wayne just needed to find the connection between Old Burt, the oak clock, and this man named Larry. The outcome of this investigation will prove to be the only way for Mr. Wayne to know how to save his wife from the hands of the curse—*he just doesn't know it yet.*

It was just a hunch, the fact that if the widow of Trego Court and Old Burt both connected to the oak clock and its enchanted curse, then it was very likely that Larry himself was suffering by the curse, too. Mainly since Old Burt was worried about Larry following him. Old Burt could've very well been talking about Larry's ghost.

So, the town's cemetery was where Mr. Wayne started with the investigation of Larry. The following day he went there intending to search every tombstone to find Larry's grave. Searching all the graves for his name was a little overwhelming for Mr. Wayne, but he wasn't about to give up. He spent an hour looking for it before he stumbled upon a grave that had a weird engraving. Mr. Wayne got on his knees to inspect the carving closely and was surprised to see that in the tombstone's carving was the word "**INNOCENT**." What a peculiar thing to carve into a tombstone, Mr. Wayne thought. When Mr. Wayne read the tombstone, he breathed a sigh of relief as the tombstone belonged to the man he sought - it was Larry's. Could this really be the same, Larry? The date of the death on the tombstone said 11th June 1901. Writing the name and the date down in his small notepad, Mr. Wayne got up and left the cemetery when he noticed the graveyard caretaker watering some plants by the gate.

Mr. Wayne walked to him and asked him if he knew anything about the man, Larry, pointing to his grave.

"Oh yes, how could I forget?" The man smirked. "Larry was the man who was wrongly convicted of killing his best friend." Mr. Wayne listened to the story attentively as the caretaker went on. "It was said that some of the old townsfolk heard Larry curse the old clock tower across from where he was burned at the stake. You might even find a few folks say that even today, when the time is right, you can see his enchanted spirit lurking around town."

"That is an unsettling story," Mr. Wayne said. But in his thoughts, everything started to click into place. Maybe Old Burt was scared about this Larry coming for him, but do mere assumptions like this hold any truth? These days this kind of incident seemed to pop up more and more, and everything was leading Mr. Wayne to believe in things that he never even considered, and did indeed exist.

Mr. Wayne thanked the caretaker and headed home. He felt like he had aged ten years in the course of this investigation.-Everything started with the old oak clock Old Burt brought into his shop. It was now obvious, the oak clock was cursed by the widow of Trego Court and the cause of all the unexplained happenings. So Mr. Wayne decided at that moment that the clock must be destroyed.

When he reached home, he was surprised to

find the door open. As Mr. Wayne cautiously entered, a feeling of dread was creeping inside of him. He closed the door behind him and called out to Mrs. Wayne, but got no response. He went inside their bedroom, and she wasn't there. Mr. Wayne became increasingly uncomfortable. He searched the library, her sewing room, the kitchen, the bathrooms, but she was nowhere to be found.

Feeling very concerned, as Mrs. Wayne had never left the house like this before, Mr. Wayne knocked on the guest room door, hoping Lisa would answer and know where Mrs. Wayne had gone.

As soon as Mr. Wayne's hand made contact with the door, it pushed open. Mr. Wayne slowly peeked inside, shocked to find that Lisa's room was empty, too. But unlike Mrs. Wayne's, Lisa's clothes and personal belongings were not in the room. *Had Lisa moved out?*

Mr. Wayne felt his legs giving out and struggled as he walked to the sofa - sitting down covering his face with his hands.

Mr. Wayne was sure in his fear that all of this was connected to the oak clock hanging quietly on their wall. Is the curse of the oak clock the reason Larry had come for Mrs. Wayne?

Time to Make Amends

Mr. Wayne was becoming very restless as he was running through all the scenarios of the past few days; feeling very uncomfortable having uncovered the enchanted mysteries of the old oak clock and the widow of Trego Court's curse. Mr. Wayne decided that the only option left was to get rid of the old clock to save his family, praying that his these actions would prove that it was not too late to put an end to these curses and more importantly, get his wife back.

Everything was starting to make more sense. Old Burt had been running from Larry for quite a while, so he must've genuinely considered Larry a threat. Mr. Wayne could not escape the thought that only a few days earlier, Old Burt mysteriously drowned in the town's well - *had Larry finally caught up with him?*

Mr. Wayne tried very hard not to think about what was happening to his wife—knowing she remained in what must be the horrible clutches of Larry. Mr. Wayne was certain about one thing; it was definitely time for Mrs. Wayne to come home.

Mr. Wayne stood up and frantically started pacing back and forth—throwing his arms up in frustration and fear, screaming with no one to hear. He needed to do something, and he needed to do it now. He could no longer sit back and let Mrs. Wayne suffer the wrath of the curse that had nothing to do with this gentle lady.

Surely the curse was meant for people who had done an injustice to Larry and the widow of Trego Court, Mr. Wayne thought. How could it be such a crime for Mrs. Wayne to favor an old oak clock that no one before her was prepared to take into their own home? So, no way should she be cursed or be suffering at the hands of Larry or the widow of Trego Court.

After a few minutes of intense pacing, Mr. Wayne went to his bedroom and ripped the old clock off the wall. His plan was to get the old clock as far away from his house as possible. Mr. Wayne truly believed in his heart that with the clock gone, he had a good chance of finding his wife alive and well.

Mr. Wayne then took the clock back to his shop-and put the clock on the shelf. As Mr. Wayne turned his back to the clock, all the other clocks on all the shelves came crashing down. The rumble of thunder that followed caused Mr. Wayne to jump away from the falling clocks, looking with disbelief at the pile of broken wood and glass before him.

"What the heck is happening here?" Mr. Wayne cried.

Just then, Mr. Wayne heard a growling voice coming from the shelf above him.

"You will never get your wife back!"

Mr. Wayne looked up to find the old oak clock sitting on the shelf unscathed.

Mr. Wayne knew now more than ever that he needed to get rid of the clock immediately. Would destroying the clock mean the removal of

Larry's curse, and if Larry's curse no longer existed, then what would become of Mrs. Wayne? Mr. Wayne had to make the biggest decision of his life—was he truly ready to take such a risk with the life of his wife? Was this the only way to get his wife back safe and sound?

In the end, Mr. Wayne knew that since Larry was the one that had taken Mrs. Wayne, Larry was the one to give her back.

Mr. Wayne grabbed the old oak clock off the shelf. He thought hard to think of where he could find Larry. A moment later, it clicked. There was only one place where Mr. Wayne would find Larry, the town's cemetery.

With the clock clutched tightly in his hands, Mr. Wayne closed the shop and took the nearest bus to the town's cemetery. He knew he had to hurry, as time was running out for his wife.

Mr. Wayne took no time to hop off the bus as it stopped in front of the cemetery and then headed straight to Larry's grave site. On the way to the site, Mr. Wayne picked up a shovel that he noticed earlier lying against a grave marker, along with some other gardening tools.

Thankfully, no one stopped him on the way, and as soon as Mr. Wayne was in front of Larry's grave, he started digging. He knew he needed to be quick, praying that no one would discover him digging up an old grave.

Nearly exhausted and out of breath, Mr. Wayne continued digging and after a foot deep, Mr. Wayne felt something beneath the dirt. He threw the shovel aside and started digging frantically with his hands.

When a toe emerged from under the dirt, Mr. Wayne recoiled in fear. His heart almost stopped with the realization of what he had assumed was actually true.

Mrs. Wayne was buried in the same grave site as Larry!

With tears falling from his eyes, Mr. Wayne dug out his wife from under the dirt, her eyes closed and not breathing. Mr. Wayne checked her for a pulse—administered CPR while the tears fell from his eyes.

With a gasping breath of life, Mrs. Wayne responded. She was still alive.

Mr. Wayne pulled her out of the grave she had shared with Larry. Mr and Mrs. Wayne stood together as he threw the old oak clock inside Larry's grave.

"Honey?" she whispered, "Is it over?"

Mr. Wayne turned to Mrs. Wayne at the sound of her voice, with a feeling like he was seeing her for the first time. As he carefully wiped the dirt off her face, Mr. Wayne kissed Mrs. Wayne, hugging her as if he would never let her go.

"You're safe now... It is all over...," he whispered in her ear.

"Can we go home now?" Mrs. Wayne asked, looking into Mr. Wayne's eyes.

"Yes, soon dear, but first we must set some wrongs things right."

With that, Mr. Wayne took out his bus ticket and a lighter from his pocket. Lighting the bus ticket on fire, he threw it on the oak clock—it didn't take but a minute for the clock to ignite.

"Here you go, Larry!" Mr. Wayne called out. "Here's the clock with which you tormented so many innocent lives. It's all yours. Let this be the end of your curse and that of the widow of

Trego Court,"

After watching it burn for a few minutes, and was sure that the clock was destroyed, he and Mrs Wayne turned to leave the cemetery and go back home. Just as Mr. and Mrs. Wayne reached the cemetery gates, the caretaker appeared from around the corner and greeted Mr. Wayne.

"Good evening folks, do you remember me, I'm Samuel, the caretaker? Everything good, folks?" he asked politely.

"Yes," said Mr. Wayne with a smile. "Everything is okay now."

Mrs. Wayne then turned to Mr. Wayne and with a nervous look on her face asked, "Is it?"

A Grandfather's Love

When Mr. and Mrs. Wayne returned home completely exhausted, both were still in shock about the day's events. Mrs. Wayne remained in disbelief that Larry had actually buried her alive in his grave. Mr. Wayne couldn't stop thinking about how close the old oak clock had almost destroyed the love of his life. He truly believed that it was by the grace of God alone that allowed him to discover his wife's whereabouts before she perished. He tried not to think about what might've happened had he been one more minute late to save his wife.

"Let's just call it a night," Mr. Wayne said as he sat down next to his wife on the sofa - pouring himself a glass of water from the pitcher on the coffee table.

"I should take a bath before bed." Mrs. Wayne whispered somewhat to herself, realizing she was covered in dirt from head to toe.

"Yes, you are a bit stinky, my dear," Mr. Wayne replied with a gentle smile. A smile not received well by Mrs. Wayne, based on the stern frown coming from her face.

Mrs. Wayne suddenly stood up and began running from room to room with a frenzied expression on her face. In less than a minute, she had checked the entire house, ending right back where she started, in the living room with Mr. Wayne.

"Where are Lisa and baby Julie?" she asked Mr. Wayne in a frantic voice.

Gulping down the rest of his water, Mr. Wayne sat up a little straighter.

"Honey, I really don't know where Lisa and Julie are." he explained as he sat the glass down and stood up to embrace Mrs. Wayne.

"They were both gone when I came home earlier and discovered you were missing. Did Lisa not say anything to you about her and baby Julie leaving?"

Tears started falling from Mrs. Wayne's eyes as she began to speak. "No, Lisa never said a word to me, and with all that has happened, she may not have had a chance to. I refuse to believe that Lisa would ever leave us without saying a word."

"Do you remember anything she may have told you that might have indicated a reason for them to want to leave?" Mr. Wayne asked, as he wiped her tears.

"No, nothing. Other than that, she and baby Julie were really happy to be here with us. But I remember having a feeling that she was scared about something. She never told me what exactly what it was she was afraid of though." Mrs. Wayne answered as she continued concentrating on remembering.

I wonder what could have put that poor girl in such a state of mind. What was she so afraid of?—Mr. Wayne's mind was racing with questions as Mrs. Wayne was recounting the day's events.

"There was one conversation we had where Lisa told me she thought someone was following her every time she and baby Julie left the house. Come to think of it, when I went out to get the groceries today, Lisa and baby Julie were nowhere to be found, so I went alone, Oh my lord, do you think?" Mrs. Wayne trailed off, gazing into the distance.

"Honey, go take your bath. We can talk more about this in the morning." Mr. Wayne watched his wife leave the room as he already feared the worst. Lisa thought someone was following her. Had Larry somehow gotten to her, too? Mr. Wayne knew he needed to find Lisa and baby Julie. Perhaps there are clues in her room that might lead to her whereabouts.

Mrs. Wayne returned from her bath shaking and dripping wet, with nothing more than an old blue robe wrapped around her.

"Honey, what's wrong, I thought you were in bed. You look like you have seen a ghost." Mr. Wayne said, realizing he could have chosen his words more carefully. Mr. Wayne went to his wife and held her tightly to stop her from shaking.

"No, I can't sleep right now." Mrs. Wayne freed herself from Mr. Wayne. "We need to find out what has happened to Lisa and baby Julie and we need to do it right now," she yelled as she rushed to Lisa and baby Julie's room, Mr. Wayne following close behind. She started rummaging through her things. Tossing the bed sheet aside, looking behind the furniture, and even turning over the mattress, when she noticed Lisa's shoulder bag hidden behind the long and black curtains.

Mr. Wayne asked Mrs. Wayne to open the bag quickly. When she did so, inside, she found baby Julie's clothes, washed and folded, as if ready to be taken somewhere.

Mr. Wayne was the first person to break the silence. "It looks like she was planning on leaving after all."

"No, she didn't." Mrs. Wayne scolded Mr. Wayne as she looked up at him. "If she had left, why would she leave the clothes behind? There is obviously something very wrong going on here."

At that moment, Mrs. Wayne heard a faint sound coming from within the house.

"Did you hear something?" she asked Mr. Wayne as he edged closer to the door to listen. Mr. Wayne walked into the hall to see if he could tell where the sound was coming from.

They both stood in the darkened hallway in silence, listening for what now appeared to be an enchanted chiming, a gentle sound that continued when Mrs. Wayne spoke up.

"It's coming from the basement. Let's go see." Mr. and Mrs. Wayne rushed to the basement, navigating the steep stairs with the skills of a cougar. Mr. Wayne looked proudly at his wife, realizing how brave and determined she was, especially after just going through such a traumatizing event.

As Mr. and Mrs. Wayne walked hand-in-hand, each careful step brought them nearer to the elegant chiming that now could be heard throughout the house. As they continued their frightful but determined journey across the basement, the sound became louder and louder. They both could now hear that the sound was indeed the enchanted chimes coming from an old grandfather clock. A grand old grandfather clock that was stored in the basement decades ago.

Mr. and Mrs. Wayne found themselves in the basement's corner, standing in front of the grand old grandfather clock, staring at its majestic beauty. They were both surprised to see the grand old grandfather clock ticking away with gentle ease and precision. Suddenly, without warning, Mrs. Wayne let out a terrifying scream as she looked inside the case and saw something moving. When Mr. Wayne opened the door to the grand old grandfather clock, Mrs. Wayne pulled out a wrapped up quilt. As Mrs. Wayne began to unwrap the bundled quilt, the grand old grandfather clock chimed gently as it struck on the hour, three times. With great fear and anticipation, Mrs. Wayne continued to carefully uncover what was inside the quilt. With great surprise and joy, they had found baby Julie unharmed and sleeping peacefully.

Mrs. Wayne took no time to rush baby Julie out of the basement and into Lisa's room. As baby Julie stirred a little, Mrs. Wayne feed her a bottle that was curiously inside the quilt and then rocked baby Julie gently back to sleep.

Meanwhile, Mr. Wayne remained in the basement with a very perplexed look on his face. Staring at the grand old grandfather clock and really talking to nobody, Mr. Wayne mumbled, "How did she get in there? Did Lisa put her in there?" Mr. Wayne rubbed his throbbing forehead as he recapped all the things he and his wife had experienced these past few days. The grand old grandfather clock that hadn't work for years was now keeping time and chiming in the basement, he had just rescued his wife from Larry's grave, and baby Julie was found safe and sound within the case of this grand old grandfather clock.

It appears that curses and spirits do exist. Nothing was impossible anymore. Mr. Wayne thought to himself.

Mr. Wayne joined his wife, and they began to talk about baby Julie's mother, Lisa. Mrs. Wayne spoke to her husband in a hushed tone. "I think we need to report Lisa as missing to the police. I'm afraid something horrible has happened to her."

As Mr. Wayne took out his phone to make the call, he asked in a worried tone, "Who will take care of baby Julie? Do you think the police will take her from us?"

"No, don't say anything to the police about baby Julie. Please! We can take care of her ourselves, at least until Lisa comes back," Mrs. Wayne commanded, holding the baby Julie close to her chest. Even as she spoke her words, Mr. and Mrs. Wayne knew deep inside their hearts that Lisa most likely would not be returning, both fearing that Lisa most likely has succumbed to the same fate as Old Burt.

A Lovely Clock

It was a bright and sunny day for Sam as he got ready for work at the town's cemetery as its only caretaker. Samuel had been working as an analyst for a finance company, but because of the company facing difficult times, Samuel was forced to retire early. Still, times remain tough and Sam was not all that ready to leave the work-force entirely. As fortune would have it, Sam found the caretaker's position at the town's cemetery. It was the one place where he never expected to ever work.

Despite the many rumors that had been going around about the cemetery being haunted, Samuel was not impressed. He had always been someone that would do all sorts of scary stuff just for the thrill of it all.

Samuel left his house early in the morning to catch the first bus that stopped right across from the cemetery. As there was much to do today, Sam wanted to be sure to get an early start. Sam was really looking forward to going to work, as the past few days have been a bit boring for him.

In any case, the job pays well and I sure can use the money, Sam reminded himself as he stepped off the bus and crossed the street to the cemetery.

So, through the gates he went with reserved

excitement of the new graves that needed to be prepped for the day's services.

Today was especially tiring for Sam. By the time the sun was setting, he was just finishing up with all his work. As Sam made his way back to the caretaker's office to clean up, he almost tripped over something that was barely sticking out of a grave he had stepped over. Sam pulled out whatever it was and as he pulled on it, he realized it was an old, partially charred oak clock.

Once the clock was out, Sam wondered who would've thrown a clock inside a grave? And why is the clock charred? Sam had no clue as to why the clock would have been buried, or by whom. Sam decided he could sell the clock, but first he would need to take it to the local clocksmith to get it restored; as the clock looked to be in pretty bad in condition, but repairable, he thought.

When Sam got back to the caretaker's office, he put the clock inside a cloth bag that he found in one of the drawers. Sam then waited for the weekend to visit the clocksmith located just outside of town.

Early Saturday morning, with clock in hand, Sam caught the morning bus to the clocksmith's shop, a shop that he hadn't been to in a very long time. Sam stepped off the bus that left him a couple of blocks away from the shop.

"Good morning. How can help?" the clocksmith greeted Sam as he walked through the door. Sam was surprised to see a much younger person behind the counter—not at all what he remembered from his last visit to the store many years ago.

Without saying a word, Sam took the old clock out of his bag, put it on the counter in front of the clocksmith, and began to carefully unwrap the clock.

"Wow, looks like your clock may need a bit of work." the clocksmith politely remarked.

"Yea, I'm really here to hopefully sell this clock. What do you think I would need to do to get a good price for it? Is it even worth restoring?" Samuel rambled on in the shadow of embarrassment.

"Looking at the condition of the clock, I would say it's always better if you get the clock repaired before selling it," the clocksmith replied. "And I believe that this old oak clock would sell at a price that could get you a new clock."

"Well, I really need the money. I actually don't need another clock. I just need to sell this one. Would you be interested in purchasing the clock from me as is?" Samuel finally asked.

"Well, I'm afraid I won't be able to give you much for it since it's in such a battered condition. It would take a lot work to fully restore this clock to its original condition."

Only then could I sell it for a price worth my time, the clocksmith said to himself.

"What could you offer?" Samuel asked with a pause.

The clocksmith took a few moments to really look at the clock. The clocksmith examined the case and movement - a full restoration would require all of his talent.

"The best I could offer would be..." and before the clocksmith finished, Sam jumped in with, "I'll take it!"

The clock had been sold to the clocksmith, and Samuel took the next bus home a few dollars richer with a smile on his face.

The clocksmith was equally happy, too, since he knew he had landed a great deal. He had already realized that the clock was not an ordinary one, but one made of fine material and, with some effort, will be good as new.

Soon after Sam left the shop, the clocksmith went right to work. The first thing that was done was to rebuild the movement, repairing both the time and strike mechanisms. Now it was time for the restoration of the case, a far more daunting task because of the mysterious charring. The clocksmith crafted new pieces that replaced the wood, then with precision of a surgeon, cleaned and polished the case until it looked as good as it did the day it was built 100 years ago. When the clocksmith turned the clock around to its face to wind it up, he noticed the initials "PL" beautifully engraved on the inside of the case.

What an interesting carving, the clocksmith

thought.

Finished, the clocksmith was proud of the restoration and how elegantly beautiful the old clock looked. There is always a special place in the shop to sell a clock like this, so the clocksmith put the old oak clock on the middle shelf in the display case - in the clear view of everyone who visits.

The shop saw many visitors over the next few days—some folks would come in just to gaze at the clock that caught their eye as they were passing by. Many people came in and left. Only a few would inquire about the price of the old oak clock, but that was as far as their interest would take them. The clocksmith was getting a little frustrated with the fact that the clock was not yet sold.

"So much time and effort and still the clock isn't sold." the clocksmith would mumble with each failed visit.

Then one day, the clocksmith's fortune would be realized. Ms. Alyce was walking by when she caught a glance of the clock sitting in the case—it was as if the clock had called out to her to come into the shop. Without hesitation, Ms. Alyce bought the clock and thanked the clocksmith for the quality of the restoration.

Ms. Alyce was an elegant lady who lived alone in a humble estate. The townsfolk, even today, remain curious about how much wealth she may have being a widow four times over. The town's children grew up being told stories by their parents about the old estate and the lady who lived there—the result was that most of the town's people avoided the old estate and sadly, Ms. Alyce, at no fault to to Ms. Alyce, some thought her to be the widow of Trego Court..

When Ms. Alyce made her way home, she carefully placed the clock on a shelf in her bedroom, the same room where she spent most of the day. Ms. Alyce sat down in her chair to admire the old oak clock with great comfort.

It had been quite a while since she had become so attached to anything, let alone an old oak clock. She just couldn't seem to let go of a feeling she hadn't felt for a very long time. The lovely chimes of the clock that echoed throughout the silent room were music to her ears.

For the first time in her life, Ms. Alyce was able to get a good night's rest. Aware that the clock was so close to her, Ms. Alyce felt very comfortable sleeping on the floor right under the clock - never understanding or questioning the attraction she was feeling towards the old oak clock.

Ms. Alyce had never felt true happiness in her lifetime and had long since given up trying to search for it until she came across the old oak clock. With it around, she felt joyous, and safe.

Days passed by, all the same as the previous ones, until one day, the clock surprised Ms. Alyce as she was falling asleep on the floor, once again, under the clock—startled as she was awakened by a husky voice calling out to her.

"Alyyyce…," the voice whispered.

Ms. Alyce had never heard the voice of

another in her home for over 20 years.

"Alyyyce…" the voice once again called out.

Ms. Alyce looked around here and there and got scared when she realized that the voice came from somewhere very close—somewhere above her?

"I'm right here, Alyce. It's okay! Don't be afraid." the voice commanded in a servient tone.

Her face quickly turned to face the clock, as it finally became clear to her.

The voice was coming from the clock! The clock was talking to her?

"Am I going crazy or are you really speaking to me?" Ms. Alyce asked in a frantic voice.

"No, Alyce. You're not crazy, I am the

enchanted spirit that you have long awaited for." the clock whispered again.

Ms. Alyce and the old oak clock engaged in a long conversation throughout the night and into morning. Finally, Ms. Alyce laid back down on the floor as the clock began chiming beautifully, and Ms. Alyce fell into a deep sleep.

Spirit Mates

As the afternoon sun shined brightly on Ms. Alyce's face, there was a refreshed look of renewal that had been missing for years. As Ms. Alyce was waking up, stretching her arms out above her head, she gently bumped the clock she was laying under. Ms. Alyce stood up, looking directly into the face of the clock, as she started to remember the conversations between her and the clock last night. *Or was it all a dream?* Ms. Alyce asked herself.

The moment Ms. Alyce turned away from the clock, a voice from the clock stopped her in her tracks; as she now prayed that her conversations with the clock last night were nothing more than a dream.

"Good day, Ms. Alyce, how are you this lovely afternoon?" the voice politely asked Ms. Alyce.

"Dear Lord, I am going crazy!" Ms. Alyce shouted at the clock.

"No... No... you're absolutely fine, Ms. Alyce?" the old oak clock replied.

Still in disbelief, Ms. Alyce looked around, confused and scared, as it took a few moments for her to accept that the voice was really coming from the old oak clock and not inside her head. At this moment, Ms. Alyce faced the realization that last night wasn't a dream.

"May I ask your name? You do have a name, don't you?" Ms. Alyce asked hesitantly.

"Yes, of course you can. My name is Larry." The clock answered with a deep and husky voice.

To Ms. Alyce, the voice made her feel as if a man was in the room. A gentle smile formed on Ms. Alyce's face as she dragged her chair closer to the clock, if for no other reason than to sit closer so that not a word was missed between them.

"Tell me about yourself," she asked in a cautious whisper.

Ms. Alyce became enchanted with the deep and husky voice of the old oak clock. Her anticipation for the next conversation overwhelmed her patience—Ms. Alyce would do all she could to encourage the next engagement between her and the old oak clock. As the days went on, so did the conversations. They became longer and much more intimate. Ms. Alyce held nothing back with the old oak clock. Their relationship grew stronger and stronger and always ending in a gentle melody that would put Ms. Alyce into a deep sleep - Ms. Alyce would always find herself falling asleep under the clock.

For the first time in her life, Ms. Alyce didn't feel lonely. She had spent so many years devoid of any human contact, and now she was making up for it. It didn't matter to Ms. Alyce that the clock wasn't human. To her, she considered the enchanted spirit of the old oak clock human enough. Ms. Alyce had grown so attached to the voice of the old oak clock that she spent every minute of the day by its side.

Her life revolved around the clock. She held no reserve in taking its advice in every matter—trusting the old oak clock so much that there was no doubt that she would blindly entrust the clock with her life. On one particular day, the clock made a very peculiar request to Ms. Alyce, a request that even she had to think twice about before responding.

"The cemetery, Ms. Alyce, may we go there?" the clock asked.

"Heavens, what on earth for?" Ms. Alyce quickly replied.

The clock answered, "I believe I may have a way for us to always be together for eternity."

Ms. Alyce could not believe what the clock was proposing. "Together forever. How?" she asked.

As the clock spoke the words, "Ms. Alyce, you must trust me. It is possible if it is something you wish to happen.". Ms. Alyce was filled with anticipation of what this could mean. *Could the old oak clock be telling me the truth?* She thought carefully before speaking her next words - "If going to the cemetery will keep us together, then let us not waste any more time"

It was as if Ms. Alyce's soul was possessed. She couldn't refuse anything that the old oak clock asked of her. So, she wrapped the clock in a soft cotton quilt that she had taken off the bed and and caught the next bus to the town's cemetery.

Ms. Alyce hopped off the bus and ran across the street to the grand entrance of the cemetery. Once inside, Ms. Alyce heard a faint voice coming from inside the quilt. "Ms. Alyce, we to need find our way to an old grave site." Ms. Alyce obeyed the clock as it continued to tell her where to go. She walked a few quick steps forward, then turned left and a few more steps then turned right, ran forward a few yards, just as the voice under the quilt was instructing her to do.

Suddenly, Ms. Alyce found herself standing in front of an old grave marker. The carving read REST IN PEACE ~ LARRY.

"Ms. Alyce, we are almost there. You must start digging," the clock demanded. Ms. Alyce unwrapped the clock from the quilt and placed it carefully next to the grave marker. She then placed the quilt on the ground over the grave to protect her knees when she knelt down and started to dig with her bare hands. She found the ground to be unusually soft as she made her way down. Ms. Alyce lost all time as she kept digging deeper and deeper until she felt something touch her fingers. That was when the old oak clock once again spoke up.

"Ms. Alyce, you made it, you're there. Now clear the lid and open my casket."

Ms. Alyce brushed the remaining dirt away from over the lid of the casket, struggling to open the lid as it was old and crusted. After a few minutes, she finally opened the lid. Ms. Alyce let out a horrific scream when she exposed the skeletal remains inside.

"Ms. Alyce, it's OK, don't be scared. Your fears will soon pass and we will be together forever.", were the comforting words Ms. Alyce heard from the deep and husky voice of the clock.

The clock continues with its enchanted verse, accompanied by its gentle chimes.

"Now, come lay down beside me Alyce."

Ms. Alyce reached up above the grave to take the clock as she carefully laid down inside the casket, with more comfort than fear, next to the skeletal remains of Larry.

"Now close the lid and close your eyes." the clock commanded.

Ms. Alyce extended her hand above her, took hold of the lid, and forced it closed, leaving her, the clock, and the skeleton in complete darkness.

"Now we are united forever and eternity,"

the old oak clock spoke in a chilling tone.

Laying in darkness in complete silence, Ms. Alyce snapped her out of her trance. She opened her eyes, but she could not see a thing. She could still feel the clock in her hands, but heard no voice and no chimes. The clock felt lifeless. In a panic, with her heart pounding, Ms. Alyce tried to push open the lid, but it wouldn't budge.

It wasn't long before Ms. Alyce felt herself becoming breathless and anxious about where she was and how she was going to get out. No matter how hard she tried, it seemed like the casket was never going to open. It was as if the lid was being held closed by Larry himself.

She kept screaming for help, pushing the lid with all her might, but in vain. Her voice was now too weak to be heard by anyone—except for maybe Larry. Ms. Alyce stopped with all of her screaming and her attempts to open the casket. As the air inside the casket began to run out, Ms. Alyce made one final plea to the voice of the old oak clock. "Larry, please, let me go…".

The silence was broken by the soft and gentle chiming of the old oak clock. For the final time, the voice from the clock told Ms. Alyce, "Alyce, it's all going to be alright now, we are finally together for forever and eternity."

Soon, the silence returned as Ms. Alyce laid still and motionless. The old oak clock turned to smoke, disappearing altogether. At this moment,

Larry finally found his peace and, perhaps reluctantly and unwillingly, Ms. Alyce found her spirit mate.

You see, in the most uncommon fashion and the least of anyone's expectations, once the two souls of Larry and Alyce were brought to together, the evil rampage of Larry and the curse of Trego Court were both lifted.

God bless, Mom, I love you more…

The End

Don't Look Into The Well...

Sleep Tight...